THE ASSISTANT

A BAD BOY BILLIONAIRE ROMANCE

MICHELLE LOVE

CONTENTS

	Sign Up to Receive Free Books	1
1.	Chapter 1	3
2.	Chapter 2	9
3.	Chapter 3	14
4.	Chapter 4	18
5.	Chapter 5	22
6.	Chapter 6	28
7.	Chapter 7	33
8.	Chapter 8	37
9.	Chapter 9	42
10.	Chapter 10	49
11.	Chapter 11	55
12.	Chapter 12	61
13.	Chapter 13	65
14.	Chapter 14	69
15.	Chapter 15	74
	Sign Up to Receive Free Books	80

Made in "The United States" by:

Michelle Love

© Copyright 2020 – Michelle Love

ISBN: 978-1-64808-234-4

ALL RIGHTS RESERVED. No part of this publication may be reproduced or transmitted in any form whatsoever, electronic, or mechanical, including photocopying, recording, or by any informational storage or retrieval system without express written, dated and signed permission from the author

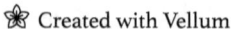 Created with Vellum

SIGN UP TO RECEIVE FREE BOOKS

Sign Up to Receive Free E-Books and Audiobook Codes.

WOULD you like to read **Savage Hearts** and **other romance books** for **free**?

YOU CAN SIGN up to receive free e-books and audiobooks by typing this link into your browser:

HTTPS://IVYWONDERSAUTHOR.COM/IVY-WONDERS-AUTHOR

BLURB

Lust. Lies. Power

For Brock Gordon, the biggest playboy billionaire in the entire country, it's just another day. When he sees something he wants, he gets it, no matter what—or who—it is. Life has always been one big game for Brock, and he knows he can have anything in the world if he waits for it.

Until he meets a young girl who is fresh out of college.

She is everything Brock never knew he wanted. She is young, she is fresh, she is so innocent to the ways of the world of men.

And she has spirit.

From the moment he lays his eyes on her, he knows that he has to have her. But this prey is proving much harder to catch, and for the first time in his life, Brock must come to terms that he doesn't get everything he wants.

Or does he?

CHAPTER 1

"Say what?"

The meeting room, previously full of light chatter as the various executives waited to get things underway, went silent.

Brock met Jennie Gray's eyes, the woman looking more defiant than contrite. "What do you mean, Andrew Vetter isn't phoning into the meeting?"

Jennie, a temp worker hired specifically to help out with such matters, shrugged. "It means he's not phoning in. Is that a problem?"

"Uh ... yeah," Brock said dryly. "He's the whole point behind this meeting. We literally have nothing to do here without his input."

For the first time, Jennie looked flustered. "Um. Oh. I didn't—"

"I'm aware. I probably didn't make it clear." It was all Brock could do not to yell in frustration, but it really wasn't the woman's fault. She was being asked to hold together all the various pieces of his business life, without the benefit of a title, a commensurate salary, or even any kind of training. Maybe someone with the right kind of mentality could have run with the job as a temp and landed a good position with Brock in the long-term. Jennie, however, clearly wasn't interested.

He directed his look at the silent executives. "Sorry for wasting your time, folks. I'll call another meeting in a few days, as soon as I coordinate a day with Vetter."

The chatter started up again as people stood and began to gather their papers, coffee, and donuts. Jennie had at least coordinated those three things well, including the agenda. Of course, the agenda clearly read Edward Vetter Meeting, so you'd figure she might have guessed ...

Brock stifled a sigh and turned to Jennie, who had resumed her defiant stance in the seat beside his. "We need to talk."

Thirty acrimonious minutes later, Jennie was headed back to the temp agency with a generous stipend to make up for the days on her contract she wouldn't complete. Brock hadn't gotten where he was by walking all over people. Be good to them, they'd be good to you down the road, he'd learned.

And as she left the building, he entered his office and rolled his shoulders. Jennie had offered some good parting advice.

Hire a personal assistant. Some young kid who you train to your managerial style. A coffee getter, paper pusher, meeting scheduler, whatever.

But who? Brock wondered as he took a seat at his vast desk, pushing aside the stacks of paper that seemed to multiply in his absence. Bitcoins were the new thing, which was proving to be both a curse and a blessing. All the young kids wanted to get in on them, but no one understood how they worked. It was a perfect storm of the greatest idea on the planet, combined with roadblock after roadblock.

For a time, he'd managed to do it all, minus outside assistance. But with the sudden surge in interest, all the balls he was juggling were about to come crashing down unless he got a second pair of hands to help him manage the back end of things.

Irritated, Brock grabbed the laptop that was sitting in front of him and opened it, pulling up the biggest job service site in the city. It wasn't how he usually found his employees, but there was no time to waste on extended interviews at this stage. He needed someone, yesterday.

"ERICA, IT JUST MAKES SENSE," Meagan began, gesturing in the direction of the In and Out around the corner, the one they both spent way too much time at. Now Meagan was suggesting Erica spend even more time there, wearing a uniform.

"Shut up! I'm not going to work fast food! I didn't go thousands of dollars into debt to dish up fries!" Erica Samson rolled her eyes.

Meagan crossed her arms. "You're thousands of dollars in debt. Dishing up fries at least also dishes up some money ..."

The words stung, but Erica brushed them off. "If I try to pay off my college debt by working at a fast food joint, I'll be dead before my loans are paid."

Meagan gave her friend a look of disapproval. They'd been friends for years, had recently graduated from college together, and this was the most they'd ever argued.

Meagan thought that they should both find any job that they could and start bringing in some money while Erica felt living in Chicago would make it easy for her to find a job in her field, and she wasn't going to waste her time on a job that wasn't taking her down the road to her dreams of being a successful accountant.

Unfortunately, that meant she had been sleeping on Meagan's couch for the past few months, and she was just as ready to get out of the crowded apartment as her friend was ready for her to go. She had been giving Meagan as much money as she could afford to spare, to pay for her bunking in the living room, but the tension was growing between them. If she didn't get out of the apartment soon, Erica knew their long friendship might not survive.

She looked away from Meagan, back to the computer, and scrolled down another row on Monster.com. To her surprise and delight, up popped:

Future Enterprises

Urgent: Seeking secretary.

"Look! Here's something!" Erica pointed and Meagan came over, sitting cross-legged on the couch with her cup of coffee in her hands.

"What is it?"

"It's a secretarial job. Not accounting, but I'd rather serve staples and office memos than Diet Cokes. I've never heard of this place before, though. Future Enterprises?" Erica looked up from the screen at her friend, who looked just as confused as she was. Suddenly, there was a flash of recognition in Meagan's face.

"I know what that is! The guy's name is Brock Gordon, and he established some sort of Bitcoin bank or something. He's looking for a secretary? Apply!" She pointed to the ad, running her fingers across the lines and looking at her friend.

In spite of her momentary excitement, Erica frowned. Her stubbornness was both her best and worst quality. "I don't know. It's not accounting."

"Erica," Meagan groaned. "Are you kidding? It's a major financial firm, so consider it a stepping stone. Not to mention you'd be working for one of the richest men in Chicago, if not the world. The guy's a billionaire. Think of the bonuses." Meagan nudged her with her elbow, and Erica hesitated.

"It's not really the same thing," she started to argue, but Meagan cut her off.

"Apply! It's not a restaurant, and you'll be making good

money if you get it. Who knows? He might have something available that you do want to do, but you're never going to know if you don't apply." Meagan got off the couch, skillfully rising without spilling her coffee on either herself or the floor. Erica watched as her friend rose, then went back to the screen in front of her.

"What makes you think he's going to hire me? He's got quite a list here of the things that he's looking for. I doubt a twenty-two year old college graduate is going to make the cut."

"You're hot. That might help," Meagan replied with a sly wink as she walked over to the kitchen, kicking aside a pile of Erica's dirty laundry as she did.

"Meagan!"

"What? I'm just saying. Use what you've got. If you don't have the credentials, use your assets." Meagan smiled then set her mug on the counter. "Anyway, you need a job, and I need a shower. And maybe my couch back at some point this century. When I get back out here, I want to hear that you've applied."

"Yes, Mother," Erica said dryly. Meagan gave her another look on her way to the bathroom. After she disappeared from view, Erica sank into the couch with another sigh.

Is this really what it's coming down to? My looks instead of my brains?

She didn't even believe that she was hot. Attractive, perhaps, but certainly not hot enough to get a job based on that fact. She had auburn red hair cut close to her head on one side and longer on the other, edgy for a secretary, but she could pull it back and hide the fact she had it short on the side. She was short, but of an athletic build, and commanded the attention of everyone in the room.

Erica knew how to work what she had, but she didn't think it would work on a man like Brock Gordon, even if she dared attempt it. Now that she thought about it, she had heard of him;

a billionaire in his thirties who had been made rich with a good idea. He was like the next Bill Gates, only better.

It didn't matter what she looked like. She'd have to be a celebrity if she was going to rely on anything but her education to get her a job at a place like that.

But then, it certainly didn't hurt to try.

What was the worst that could happen? And after he found her attractive and hired her, then she could put her brain front and center. Right?

CHAPTER 2

"I just want to know what's taking so long? Who wouldn't want to work for my company? Or me, for that matter?" Brock muttered. It had been only three days since he had put the listing on the job service website, but he'd expected that there would be more applicants than what they were already getting.

"We're working on it, but I can only talk to those who have come through," Angie said. "It's not like nobody's applied. You're just so freaking picky." She didn't bother hiding her annoyance with Brock. But then, no one did. He had the kind of relationship with his employees that allowed them to talk to each other in such a way without worrying about any tension.

"More should apply," Brock grumbled. "I reserve the right to be picky about the people I'm trusting with my company!"

"The next applicant is supposed to be here in an hour!" she called after him as he stormed off toward his office. "The résumé's on your desk, along with her references!"

"Call them and see if they can get in here sooner," he said. He didn't wait for an answer, heading off to his office. As Angie had said, there was a crisp one-sheet resume on the desk and he scanned it.

Erica Samson

She was young, recently graduated, but her various internships had been high level, with some well-known people in the field listed as contacts who would vouch for her work ethic. She'd graduated with honors, too.

Hmm. Could be overqualified. Could be under. Hard to tell with someone so fresh out of school.

He wanted someone who would be able to handle all that he was going to throw their way, but he also wanted someone he could work with. Someone who could put up with him without getting butt hurt about the way he treated them. He wasn't a patient man. That was just fact. Patience hadn't built his billions.

"She's here," the voice came through the intercom, and Brock opened his eyes in surprise.

"You said an hour!"

"And you said tell her to get here sooner and she was just around the corner," Angie shot back. "Do I send her away?"

"Don't be ridiculous. Send her in."

A moment later, Angie opened the door to the office and just like that, in walked the most beautiful woman Brock had ever seen.

He stared in total shock, not sure what he'd expected, but certainly not this. She was petite, with gorgeous red hair cut in a seriously sexy style that somehow made her look both soft and edgy at the same time. There was no hiding the fact that she was in good shape, her lithe curves poured into a gray suit that couldn't come close to containing that toned body.

Then there were her eyes, sparking intelligent blue fire in his direction, and he realized he'd been standing there stupidly, gawking.

"Hello! Miss Samson, come on in and have a seat!" Brock said hastily.

"It's so nice to meet you," she said, not nearly as nervous as any of the other applicants as she walked forward. Her stride was sure and her handshake was firm and steady as their fingers met. Brock felt a powerful jolt of heat and barely contained a groan.

Beautiful and confident? Oh, yes. Now if we can just pair that with some outstanding secretarial abilities ...

Though she didn't know his name, he decided on a whim not to give it to her. He already liked her, and he didn't want to make her even more uncomfortable by finding out he was the man who owned the entire business. Instead, he decided to plunge directly into the interview and see how things went with her.

"I looked over your résumé, and I am quite impressed," he said.

She smiled, obviously pleased. "Thank you."

"I have to ask right away—having worked with such high level companies, why take a secretarial position now?" Brock deliberately threw the hardest question at her. He honestly didn't have too many more. In his position, he had learned to judge people on far less than Erica had already displayed. He liked her. He wanted her. In more ways than one, admittedly.

"They don't have any jobs," she said simply. "I could keep working for free, now that I've graduated, but that seems to make the whole degree and gazillion dollar loans a moot point."

He nodded. "Fair enough. I realize there aren't many jobs out there right now. Tight market. So you're okay with doing secretarial work? You don't see it as a step down?"

Erica grimaced. "I have to admit, I'm not quite sure about all of this, really. Obviously you know what you're doing, but I don't. They didn't teach us a thing about Bitcoins when I was in school. Honestly, it's either this or a burger joint, by the looks of things. No offense intended."

Brock flashed a wide grin. He appreciated her honesty and added it to the list of qualifications that she checked off his list.

"Well, if we hire you, I'll make sure you get some accounting experience too. It's a full-time position, and I expect all my employees to be dependable. I don't do late," he said with raised eyebrows.

"And I was an hour early to this interview," she replied with a small smile.

Oh yeah. Ohhhh, yeah. He liked her a whole lot more than he should.

"There's no need to pull punches here, Ms. Samson. I know quality when I see it. Do you have any questions for me, before we proceed?"

"How long do you think it will be before I hear back about this position? I've been living on my friend's couch for the past few months, and she's about to kill me in my sleep," Erica admitted.

"If you want the job, it's yours," Brock informed her, and for the first time, she seemed taken off guard.

"Really? I—" she began.

"And since I need my new secretary alive," he interrupted, "I'll give you the first half of your paycheck upfront." Brock smiled at the combined relief and astonishment in her beautiful eyes.

"Really?" Erica said in amazement. "I mean, thank you! I accept! I just ... I don't even know what to say. I really need the job, but I've never heard of anyone paying upfront. You trust me that much already? Doesn't Mr. Gordon need to approve me or something?"

Brock grinned. "I know Mr. Gordon extremely well. He'll approve, believe me."

Stepping around the desk, he nodded at the door and walked slightly behind her, restraining the desire to rest his hand on her lower back in a gentlemanly fashion, mostly because then he'd want to slide it lower still.

"Don't worry about a thing. I wouldn't offer it to you if it wasn't what he would want. The position needs to be filled by someone who is going to do a good job, and I can tell that someone is going to be you." He gave her a warm smile as they reached the door and he opened it for her.

"Angie! Will you please give our newest recruit the paperwork she needs?" he asked before turning back to Erica. "You'll start first thing in the morning."

"Yes, of course." Erica beamed so brightly she could've lit up a neon sign.

"Excellent! We will see you then!"

Only the phone call he had pending drew him away from his new secretary. Otherwise, he might well have stood there in the hallway, under Angie's curious, knowing gaze, trading smiles for the rest of the afternoon with Erica.

CHAPTER 3

"Oh, for fuck's sake!" Erica sighed as she ran through the door. "Late on the first day! And after I put him in his place about my being so early for the interview and all that! Oh God ... don't fire me ..."

She ran as quickly as she could through the lobby of the skyscraper and dashed straight for the stairs. No way was she waiting for the elevator! She ran all eleven flights and almost exploded into the lobby, meeting Angie's irate gaze as she stumbled, panting and red-faced, over to the desk.

"It's about time you decided to show up," Angie said without a smile. "Mr. Gordon doesn't tolerate lateness."

Erica puffed and wheezed. "I'm sorry. I left an hour ago, but I got stuck behind an accident—"

"You should have left earlier," Angie cut in coolly. "Don't let it happen again. He will not be happy. And he had me cut you that initial first half of your paycheck, too, trusting you. That's not how we do things here, Erica."

Erica flushed, if that was possible, given how red she already was.

Angie was definitely not finished raking her over the coals.

"Mr. Gordon needs his personal assistant here before him. Every day. Clear?"

That got Erica's attention. "I'm sorry. Personal what? I thought I was a secretary—"

"Secretary? Is that what he told you? You're going to be a personal assistant." Angie nodded toward the other side of the room. "Go drop your stuff off. I'll give you five minutes and then I expect you to be back here ready to work."

Erica wanted to argue, but she knew there was no point. She had been told that she was going to be the secretary, and it didn't matter now what she said. If he had told this woman that she was going to be the personal assistant, she knew there was little she could do about it. Her mind was spinning. She wanted to find that guy who had done the interview and ask him what had happened, but then, she also didn't want to see him again if she could help it.

Throughout the interview, she had done her best to keep everything as professional as possible, but she had found it incredibly difficult with how attractive the man was. He was tall, with dark hair and dark, piercing eyes. She had tried not to notice his body under his suit, but it was difficult not to.

She put her things away in the desk assigned to her, catching her breath as she did. If Erica was perfectly honest with herself, this entire place confused her. She had received a phone call the night before by someone else who worked in the company, and they had briefed her more on how the digital bank worked.

During the phone call, she had acted as though she understood everything that the man was saying to her, but the fact of the matter was that she'd had no clue. At least she'd been honest during the interview about her ignorance. They couldn't expect her to know anything Bitcoin related; she'd made it clear she was clueless.

She returned to the front desk, ready to begin her day but

not sure how her day was going to go.

As she feared, Angie was just as much of a bitch to her all throughout the morning as she had been to her from the beginning, and it wasn't long before Erica was tired of it. It quickly became clear that she couldn't do anything right—from the way she was handling the phone calls that were coming in, to the way she was handling the paperwork.

"If you can't take the pressure, get out!" Angie barked at her more than once.

Erica was so irate by the time early afternoon rolled around that she was toying with thoughts of quitting, even though that wasn't her usual style in the slightest. That, and money, stalled the impulse.

"Hey! How's it going?" a man's voice broke into her thoughts, and both she and Angie looked up. Erica noticed that she quickly looked down again, but her mind was quickly caught up in the fact that the incredibly handsome man who had interviewed her was leaning on the desk.

"Fine." Was Angie's one-word reply.

"I didn't know I was going to be a personal assistant," Erica informed him. "The job post said secretary."

The man lifted one broad shoulder and flashed her a melting grin. "The interview went so well that we decided we'd upgrade the job, and the salary."

That gave Erica pause. "Okay ... I guess. The day just hasn't gone well," she blurted. "At all."

"I don't expect you to be perfect on your first day," he said with suddenly raised eyebrows.

"Neither do I, and I thought she was doing great. She's just being too hard on herself," Angie cut in before Erica was able to reply. Erica looked over at her and was about to say something when Angie added, "Don't worry, Mr. Gordon, she's going to be ready for anything by the time I'm done with her."

She smiled over her shoulder at Erica, and Erica's mouth dropped open.

Say what?!

Mr. Handsome himself was Brock Gordon? Billionaire and Internet genius Brock Gordon had been the one to interview her??

"You could've told me," she began, trying to steady herself from the shock and, remembering how snarky she'd been yesterday, her cheeks flamed.

"I didn't want to intimidate you," Brock said cheerfully. "You're fine. I only hire the best. Angie will show you the ropes."

"I—uh—yeah," Erica muttered totally inarticulately.

"See? Intimidation," he pointed out, and she thought she detected an amused smile hidden behind his serious face. She felt like the world's biggest idiot, but he didn't give her a chance to say anything else.

"Give yourself some time to adapt. But don't be late again," Brock warned, and with that, and a smile that took the sting off his mild rebuke, he turned to go back to his office, leaving both women to watch him as he walked away.

Erica looked over at Angie, who avoided making eye contact with her, and decided not to say anything. Nothing about this situation was making much sense to her, but she also didn't care. She didn't know what it was that had prompted him to hire her with so little experience, and she also didn't know why he hadn't told her the day before that she was going to be his personal assistant.

But, whatever his reasons, she was working for one of the richest men in the entire country, if not the entire world. Suddenly, it didn't matter how hard her day had been going so far.

She was Brock Gordon's personal assistant, and Erica decided in that moment, she was going to be the best.

CHAPTER 4

Brock lay in bed that night, staring at the ceiling, wide awake. It was a Friday, and he knew he wasn't going to see Erica again until Monday, something that made him less than happy. She had been working at the company for nearly three weeks, and he felt that he had done an excellent job of behaving himself around her, however hard it had been. Hard being the operative word.

He was a playboy, no denying it. Work hard, play hard, love harder yet. He was honest about it, never leading women on about his lack of interest in anything but some time between the sheets.

But he couldn't get Erica off his mind. The outfits she wore were almost more than he could bear, especially when he was in his office and she would come and lean over his desk. It wasn't like she was slutty; that might've been better. It was just that slight hint of demure cleavage, the curve of her tight backside in her nicely fitted slacks or dresses ... More than once he had imagined throwing her down over his paperwork and fucking her from behind, imagining how she would moan and writhe from the pleasure of it all.

Yet he also knew that he had to keep things professional with her. It could quickly turn into such a scandal if he didn't play his cards right. Not to mention, there was something different about Erica. There was an innocence about her that he couldn't seem to break through. The confidence she'd displayed in the interview had fallen by the wayside when it became clear he was the Big Billionaire Boss. Her cheeks would flush when he was around; she would stumble over her words and become visibly agitated; and he enjoyed every minute of it. His alpha tendencies made him enjoy when she was clearly feeling uncomfortable, though he wished she would cut loose and be freer with herself in his presence.

She was so innocent, but he could sense that there was something under that innocence that would come out if he could just awaken it inside her. But how to do that in the workplace? That was the one domain where Brock had never made any conquests, with one exception that he now regretted. He kept his sex life strictly beyond the walls of the office.

And yet, Erica ran through his head every morning, afternoon, and worst of all, night, to the point where he was becoming seriously sleep deprived from all his lonely fantasizing. Ordinarily he would have sought another woman to relieve his need, but he suddenly wasn't interested.

In frustration, he sat up on the end of his bed, swinging his feet to the floor and running his hands through his thick black hair. Who was he kidding? He couldn't say that he was looking for the touch of any woman; he was looking for the touch of just one, the one whom he would see again bright and early Monday morning. The one whom he couldn't get off his mind right now. The one whom he would give anything just to have to himself for even half an hour.

He picked up his phone, tempted to text her. They had exchanged phone numbers, of course, since she was his personal assistant and at his beck and call. Of course, that was supposed to be strictly at work, and so far he'd held to that.

But the temptation to text was growing stronger, and with the glass of whiskey causing his brain to swim around, he didn't know if he had the willpower to say no. Setting the phone back down on the nightstand, he closed his eyes and tried to sleep.

But with no luck.

Another hour ticked by, and he looked down at his phone once more. He sighed, agitated. As a sudden impulse overtook him, he grabbed his phone and quickly typed the message before he allowed himself to think about it any further.

Great work this week. I really appreciate it!

He hit send, then looked at the clock once more and kicked himself. Talk about a lame text. And who sent something like that at one in the morning? She'd assume he was drunk, undoubtedly.

His phone chirped and he quickly grabbed it, suddenly hopeful.

But the message wasn't from her. It was from Angie.

Just wanted to let you know I still think about you from time to time. I'm sure you're in the arms of some other girl, but I want you to know what we had was special, and I'll always treasure it in my heart.

Brock groaned in dismay, regret punching him yet again.

About a year before, he and Angie had somehow fallen into bed, in spite of his no office flings rule. No denying she was a beautiful woman, and that was what he blamed it on. That and his total lack of self-control around the opposite sex.

Just like with every other woman, he'd told Angie his intentions, and to his surprise, she had accepted that and even still chosen to keep her job, even after he got bored and ended things a few days in. Perhaps she'd thought seeing her every day would change Brock's mind about her and they would get together again, or perhaps she really did like working at his company that much.

Whatever the reason, he rather wished that she would just give up on him. Nothing was ever going to happen between them again. He'd made that clear. Probably cruelly clear, but better that than lying. Why couldn't she move on?

Brock threw his phone onto the nightstand in frustration, then rolled over the other way, closing his eyes and wishing for sleep.

CHAPTER 5

"Done and done!" Erica said with triumph in her voice. She set the files down on the desk and pushed them over to Brock, who looked up at her with the familiar mischievous look he so often gave.

She felt her cheeks flush and instantly wished that they would not, knowing that he could tell every time they did. She didn't like feeling vulnerable around Brock. There was something about him that was so intimidating, she felt that he could see right through her most of the time.

"And that's why you're my favorite assistant," he said as he scooped up the papers and patted them into a neat pile.

"I'm your only assistant," Erica pointed out wryly, finally at the point where she could be around the ridiculously good-looking guy and at least hold a conversation, even if half the time it still ended in her blushing and stammering.

"If I had 10, you'd still be my favorite," Brock replied, winking, and that sent Erica into full meltdown, so she hurried made her way back to the main office.

Angie turned away as Erica walked out. The woman had apparently taken a dislike to her that just wouldn't quit. Thankfully, Erica was past the training stage, so they didn't have extended interactions any longer.

"Having fun?" Angie asked, not turning around.

"What?"

"I heard you giggling in there like a schoolgirl. I just wondered if you and your employer are having fun." Angie's tone was flat and her voice was dry, but for some reason her words made Erica's blood run cold. Though she sensed that there were always going to be problems between them, she didn't know why Angie was deciding to pick a fight with her right now.

"I wouldn't call it giggling like a schoolgirl, but yes, I do enjoy working here, thanks for asking," she said. Erica had learned that the best way to deal with Angie was to answer her attitude and move on with her own day, trying to ignore her the best she could.

"I just hope you understand that you have to be professional at work. I would hate for you to get hurt," Angie said with the same dry tone as before.

"What are you suggesting?" Erica's eyes narrowed.

"All I'm saying is that there is work etiquette and there is flirtation, and you, my friend, are walking pretty close to the line." Angie said.

Erica opened her mouth to protest, then snapped it shut. What was the point? It was probably blatantly obvious that she was attracted to Brock. No denying that. But she hadn't done anything wrong, so Angie could just think whatever she—

"Look, you're young," Angie interrupted her whirling thoughts. "I'll give you that. So I'm just telling you this because I don't want to see you get hurt. I've seen the way Brock has been with other girls, and I know that you are excited and this is all so fresh and new, but I'm warning you, it's not going to last." She turned to answer the phone.

In spite of her resolution to keep quiet, Erica opened her mouth to retort, and then her own phone beeped. She glanced at the screen and smiled.

"Is that Brock?" Angie asked, and Erica gave her a look.

"Mind your own business," she replied. She lifted the phone to her ear and retreated to a quiet part of the office where she could hear the person on the other end of the line.

"Yes, this is Erica. Yes. What? Really? No, definitely, I'm just really surprised. No, this isn't my first place, but I didn't know that they would take someone without more renting experience. I'll be down there as soon as I get off work today. Yes, thank you!"

Erica hung up the phone and looked over her shoulder. Angie was watching her, but she didn't say anything. Erica quickly looked back to her phone and slipped it into her purse.

She had just heard that she had gotten the apartment she had applied for a few weeks prior. It was ridiculously nice, and not cheap, but she could afford it on her salary. The one problem was whether they'd believe that she could make her rent, given that her bank account was still more empty than it was full. Apparently, they'd checked her references and decided she was a safe bet for a tenant!

She had to get down there to sign some paperwork, and they were going to close shortly after she got off work—so she would have to ask Brock if she could leave early.

"I'm surprised. I would have thought when they pulled my credit report that they would have said no way, but I guess they must have liked what they saw!" Erica said.

"Congratulations," Brock said with a warm smile. "I'm sure they saw what I did when you interviewed."

Angie's warning or not, Erica laughed and blushed and felt utterly teenage-girlish.

"Well, I'll see you in the morning. Thank you!" she said.

On her way down the elevator, Erica put her phone to her ear. She knew she ought to call the bank and see how much money she should transfer before she made it down to the bank, not wanting to overdraw any of her accounts. She flipped through the menu, listening to all the prompts she was being given by the computer on the other end.

She listened to the menu, but then shook her head and looked down at her phone. Something had to be wrong. Pressing the button, she listened to the entire list again. There had to be something wrong with her account. It said that she didn't have any outstanding balances of any kind.

But just the day before, she had been thousands of dollars in debt. Confused, Erica looked at her watch. She was going to have to hurry, but she would have time to stop by the bank before she went down to the rental agency.

She would have to get this straightened out.

15 minutes later, her jaw was on its way to the pavement.

"My balance is what?!"

"I TOLD you there were going to be plenty of perks for working for a billionaire!" Meagan said with a laugh, taking a pair of shoes from the store clerk and starting to try them. Erica had just told her what had happened earlier that day, and how she had had all her debt paid off.

There was no question that it had been Brock. Nobody else she knew had that kind of money. Part of Erica was thrilled, but most of her was freaked out. She couldn't stop thinking about what Angie had said, and she worried that the woman was right.

Perhaps there was more going on than what she thought—and perhaps it wasn't as innocent as she thought it was.

"Come on, you aren't sleeping with the guy, are you? I mean, it's not like you're getting perks for sex, right? Maybe he just wants to help you out, and don't tell me you don't deserve it!" Meagan said.

Erica laughed. "I don't know about that. Look at these." She held up another pair of shoes, and Meagan immediately took them from her.

Shoe shopping had seemed like at least a small way to celebrate being suddenly debt free.

"Come on, you've been through a lot, what with your dad and everything," Meagan replied.

Erica winced. It was true. She had lost her mother when she was very young, and her father had a heart condition and often required surgery. Though she didn't like to think about it, she often worried that he was going to have some kind of heart failure and would need a transplant.

"I wouldn't worry about it if I was you. That's my point." Meagan's voice broke through her thoughts, and Erica looked back over at her.

"I know how you think, Erica. It's weird. I agree. Who does that, especially for a brand-new employee?" Meagan went on. "But then again, who looks a gift horse like that in the mouth? God. I'd love a boss like ..."

She knew that her friend was right. She shouldn't worry about it. But then, she didn't want Brock to think that he owned her. She worked for him. She was his secretary. Nothing more. It was strange that he would do so much for someone who was nothing more than his assistant, and she didn't feel comfortable with what he had done.

"I don't know. I just don't want this to turn into a scandal, you know?" she asked.

"Look, if you're that worried about it, why don't you tell him so?" Meagan asked. Erica sighed. She knew her friend was right, and no matter how much she didn't want there to be tension or trouble between her and her employer, she was going to have to talk to him about this. There was just no other way.

But in the meantime ...

"Meagan ..."

Her best friend gave her a smirk. "Yeah, yeah. You're debt free. Rub it in."

"SCHOOL DEBT FREE!" Erica threw her arms around Meagan and hugged her hard. "Now I can finally pay for a new couch for you!"

Meagan laughed and hugged her back. "I wouldn't mind that. Your body pretty much permanently imprinted the cushions. But for now, I'll settle for lunch and a spa day ..."

CHAPTER 6

"I don't think it's a bad idea. I mean, I'd fuck the shit out of her if I could." Jack laughed as he downed the rest of his whiskey.

Brock looked down into his own glass.

"You better know, I'd have to fire you. And I'd probably kill you," he replied.

Jack gave him a curious look. "That's different ..."

"There is something different with this one," Brock agreed. "I mean, I wouldn't be opposed to just fucking her—God, maybe I'd finally get some sleep, then!—but I don't want to hurt her. I don't get the impression that she is very, um, experienced." Brock drained the rest of her glass and Jack gave him a look.

"Since when do you, of all people, care about that?" he asked, and Brock shrugged. The fact of the matter was that he himself didn't know when he'd started feeling that way. He had liked Erica from the moment she walked through the doors of his company, but he didn't want to hurt her. And that had honestly never much mattered to him before.

"There's just something different about this one. She's so

young. I don't want her to hate me after," he said with a light laugh.

Jack gave him another strange look, showing that he didn't know what had come over his friend. This was strange behavior for Brock, and he knew it. But, he still felt how he felt, and he wasn't going to change his mind just because he was obsessing over this girl.

"If you want to fuck her, fuck her, and don't worry about it," Jack said, and laughed as he drained his second shot.

If there was something about Jack, he could really hold his liquor, and he wasn't afraid to do it. Brock used to try to keep up with him, but not anymore; he just let his friend drink as much as he cared to and picked up the tab when they were done. At the very least, Jack was good company to talk to about things like this.

"I'll figure it out," Brock said, wondering exactly how he planned on doing that, given that he'd been trying for weeks, utterly unsuccessfully. He finished the rest of his drink then held up his hand. "Check, please!"

"I JUST DON'T FEEL comfortable with you paying that much money for me. I mean, you're already paying more than I would be making at any other place in town, and I can pay my own bills." Erica shifted back and forth in her seat, clearly nervous,

Brock, on the other hand, was sitting in his chair and smiling. He hadn't been sure how she was going to react when she learned that he had paid off her debt, and he wasn't surprised that she had reacted in the way that she did. There were some women who liked to have everything paid for them, then there were those who were upset when it happened. With the way she behaved in the office, he wasn't at all surprised that she would rather take care of things on her own.

"I understand that, and I hope you aren't offended. I didn't mean any offense by it, really. I just wanted to do something nice for you, and that was the best thing I could think of." He smiled at her as he spoke, hoping that he could calm her down with his nonchalant attitude.

She smiled, wiping her hands nervously on her skirt as she did. "I don't want you to think that I'm not grateful, because I really am. I just want you to know that I can take care of my own life. I don't need special favors."

"It wasn't special treatment, let me assure you. This was something that I do for all of my employees. Whenever anyone new starts here I make sure that they are taken care of, and what better way to do that than to take care of their debt?" he lied. He watched her keenly as he did, hoping that she would believe him, and to his relief, she appeared to.

"Really? I mean, I know that you have a lot of money, but I didn't know that you were so generous with everyone."

"I help those that I care about, and if you are in my circle, then I care about you. Simple." Brock smiled as he spoke, and she looked at him with raised eyebrows.

"All right, I'll let you do this for me once, but I want you to know that it's not something that's going to happen again." She crossed her arms and looked at him, and he gave her a strange look in return. At last, he smiled.

"Deal," Brock agreed. "I'm sorry I went behind your back. I thought it'd be a nice surprise, but I should have spoken with you first. Let me make it up to you—why don't you come out with us tonight?" He listed a few of her colleagues who were all going out with him that night.

He knew if he didn't keep talking, she might lose her nerve and decline, so he did what he could to sweeten the deal.

"It's going to be a rather quiet night for us. We're just going to grab a quick bite and some drinks after. Nothing too crazy." He winked at her, and he could see that she was clearly torn.

"What do you have to lose?" Brock urged. "When's the last time you went out and just cut loose with your friends? I mean, if you want to be friends with these people, you're going to have to get out and hang out with them from time to time." He winked at her once more, causing her to blush. He wished he could get a glimpse into what she was really thinking, but her face was as hard to read as anything he could imagine.

He was just about to give up and tell her that there was no pressure for her to go with him when he saw something change in her face. It was as though she had suddenly won a battle she had been fighting with herself, and she had made up her mind to do something that was against her better judgement.

"Well, what the hell? All right," she said after a moment of deliberation.

"Excellent. Then I want you to take this and get yourself something nice to wear." Brock reached into his wallet and pulled out his credit card, handing it to her as her eyes widened.

Erica looked at the card, then she gave him a look and shook her head. "What did we just talk about? I'm not going to be taking anymore money from you! I get my paycheck, and that is the end of that!"

"You said that gifts were fine, and that's what this is! We are going out tonight, and it's my treat."

Erica took the card before shaking her head and placing it back on the table in front of Brock. "No. I can't."

Brock opened his mouth to protest, but she was already out of her seat. "I can't, Brock. It's not professional. Besides. You pay me plenty. I'll buy a nice dress."

With a shy smile in his direction, she walked out of the room and left Brock reeling, wondering who this woman was who couldn't be bought. Who wouldn't be bought.

Damn. He really, really liked her.

CHAPTER 7

"Don't you think that it's a little strange he just gave me the card and told me to go get a dress?" Erica asked. She had stopped by her father's coffee shop on her way downtown to ask his opinion on what had been happening, but he merely shook his head.

"It's strange," her father agreed, wiping down the counter. "It's good that you didn't take it. He could get ideas. That whole debt thing ... I mean, don't look a gift horse in the mouth, but in my experience, employers just don't do that." He tossed the dish rag aside and reached for a broom to scour the empty coffee shop, the way he did whenever it was empty. She'd inherited her work ethic from him, in a big way.

She flushed, having been thinking the same thing, and took the broom from him. "Right. I really shouldn't have accepted that, but I didn't know what to do. How do you tell someone that you don't want to be debt free?"

"What's done is done," her dad went on. "Just watch yourself. He's not getting handsy or anything, is he?"

Erica turned beet red, mostly because she'd been fantasizing for weeks about him doing exactly that. "No!" she exclaimed, doing a brisk back and forth with the broom across the café's seating area, before starting on the space behind the counter. "He's always been completely professional."

"Good. As long as that continues, you're okay," her dad replied, stepping around the broom and walking over to buff the tables to a nice shine.

"He invited me out tonight," Erica mumbled, not looking at her father. Out of the corner of her eye, she saw him stop. "But we're going out with a group of people. It's not like it's a date or anything," she added quickly.

Her father gave her another look. "Just remember, if you ever feel uncomfortable with the situation or like you don't want to do something, then don't do it." He leaned over the first table and then froze, groaning quietly.

"Dad!" Erica dropped the broom and rushed over, grabbing his shoulders. He'd turned stark white.

"I'm fine." He straightened and pulled away. "I pulled a back muscle lifting something the other day. Just a spasm."

She wasn't even remotely convinced, but nagging her father never had any kind of positive effect.

"Really, I'm fine," he went on. "I want you to get out of here; you need to go find a dress." He smiled at her, but she shook her head.

"I can't leave you when you're not feeling well! I can help you close up today. You really do need at least a second person in here, Dad."

"Don't you worry about me," he said firmly. "I told you, everything is just fine here with me. Now go on, if you are going to find a dress in time for tonight, you're going to have to get started now. I know how you are, if you don't go now, you're going to be there until midnight before you even know what you're going to want," he teased.

Erica frowned. "All right," she said slowly. "But if you need anything at all—anything, Dad—you let me know."

"I always do," he reminded her, and it was true that he was good at reaching out if he needed an extra hand with something.

Still reluctant, Erica helped him finish the tables and washed a few dishes before giving him a big hug and heading out.

"I love you," she called over her shoulder and smiled at his usual response.

"I love you more, sugar sweet."

SHE DIDN'T REALLY KNOW what to expect for their outing. As Erica moved from store to store until she found the perfect emerald green dress, one that hugged her in all the right places but was modest enough that she'd be comfortable in it in any setting—it wouldn't hike up too high if she was perched on a bar stool, for instance—she built up expectations and then batted them aside. In between, she talked things over with Meagan on the phone. Down with a bad flu, her friend couldn't join her, but she offered plenty of advice anyway, ranging from earrings and shoes, hair and makeup, to the 'non-date' itself.

"You know as well as I do that this is a date-date," Meagan said yet again later on, as Erica was at home finishing up the last curls in her hair, then reaching for a necklace that matched the soft green fabric nicely.

"Yeah, yeah," Erica muttered distractedly, slipping into her new pair of heels and eyeing herself in the mirror. By now, Meagan had argued her around to accepting that this was actually more than Brock had made it appear.

"The man is into you," Meagan reminded her unnecessarily, just before hanging up. "You have to make the decision whether to pursue that or not."

It might have taken weeks for Erica to stop deluding herself, but the fact was that she and Brock did have a consistent sizzling undercurrent between them. What was the point in continuing to deny it? And if she accepted that, the question then became ... what happened next?

As the doorbell to her apartment rang, her mouth went dry and her anticipation rocketed. At the back of her mind, she made the decision right there and then. If he came onto her, she was going to go with it. If he didn't, maybe that was better career-wise. But if he did ... she was going to take the opportunity, for better or worse.

"Coming," she called, and hurried to open the door to the most handsome man she'd ever known.

CHAPTER 8

She looked like a goddess. Plain and simple. Brock almost swallowed his tongue as he escorted Erica downstairs, barely able to peel his eyes away from the dress. She might not have used his money to buy it, and it wasn't anywhere near the skimpy affair he usually liked on a woman, but it was exactly right. It left plenty to the imagination, but offered more than enough visuals—those breasts, molded to perfection within the fabric, even if the hint of cleavage was minimal; that modest stretch of leg that made him want to reach high up to explore more; that ass, for God's sake, cupped so lovingly by the dress that it made him jealous—to whet his every appetite.

"I can feel your eyes," Erica said, turning to look at him from down the hallway, and the heat in her gaze nearly froze Brock to the spot.

"You're the most beautiful woman I've ever laid eyes on," he said bluntly, not about to sugarcoat it. And when she blushed, she was even prettier. "I don't want to go out with everyone else, Erica. Point blank, I want to spend tonight with you." He let her do her own reading into that innuendo.

"I want that too."

He wasn't finished reeling from the shock of those words when she walked over and smiled up into his eyes. "This game we're playing? I don't know how it ends, but I'm enjoying it."

Brock swallowed hard, his usual total control over every facet of his life vanishing in the blink of a long, sultry eyelash. He loved how candid she was. He loved that small, slightly shy smile, the flash of her beautiful eyes, the slight huskiness to her voice. He loved her whole personality and way of being, frankly. And it scared the crap out of him how much he felt himself falling damn hard toward loving her.

Trying hard to recover his billionaire sang froid, Brock looped an arm around her waist, pulled Erica tight into his muscled chest, and gave her the full measure of his hungry gaze. "Do I kiss you now, or at the end of the date? Because it's happening today, sweetheart. That's a promise."

She bit her lip and he instantly wanting to take over biting it, running his own teeth over the soft, supple skin. "If we start now, there won't be any date. And I want a date, Brock. I want to see you outside of the office before … before," she concluded after an endearing pause that reminded him that she wasn't as confident as she always seemed to project.

Somehow, he managed to draw back without ravaging those sweet lips. "Okay," Brock said, swallowing a groan. "Then you'll get your date, honey. And possibly a whole lot more, if we both agree we'd like it."

Tentatively, she slipped her fingers into his, and though he'd never been a hand-holding guy—that seemed to imply some kind of commitment, and he was absolutely phobic in that sense—he liked how her small hand settled in his. He liked walking her out to his Lexus, holding the door for her, and waiting for her to slide into the seat. He liked leaning down to brush his lips over her cheek, because that might just hold him the rest of the night. He liked joining her in the car, climbing into the driver's seat, and finding her waiting there with her soft, by now familiar, smile.

"Pizza?" Erica asked. "I've been craving it all week. I know billionaires probably prefer more upscale ..."

"Papa John's is on speed dial," he informed her with a grin as he pulled onto the road. "I know a place."

"I've just never seen it done before," Erica insisted, walking alongside Brock with a slice of pizza in her free hand, just like he had one in his from his favorite food truck.

He drew her a little closer to his side and took a bite of his soy-sauce dipped pizza. "So it's not traditional," he said with his mouth full. "Who cares? Best stuff ever. You should try it."

She gave him a skeptical glance and took a bite of her own slice as they meandered through a park, the trees just starting to cast shadows.

It had been like this for the last 45 minutes, from the drive to the food truck to the park. Sizzling with chemistry, even as they talked about everything. Brock had learned more about Erica's background in those 45 minutes than he had in all the time she'd been working with him, and his admiration had only grown as he found out how she'd worked her way through college, paying both her own bills and her father's medical bills somehow simultaneously. He'd even shared some of his own story, which he didn't talk much about, growing up with two less than doting parents, leaving home young and clawing his way up to his current position in the financial world.

"Tell me one more time," Erica urged, and he laughed. In the midst of telling their life stories, she'd also found time to press him about how exactly Bitcoin worked.

"Each transaction is associated with a hash. In a block, each transaction hash is also hashed, sometimes more than once, and the final product is the Merkle root. It's the root of the hash of all hashes—"

She groaned. "Leaves. Nodes. Roots. Whoever created the system had a tree fetish!"

Brock grinned, fully aware that as smart as Erica was, she'd understand the complexities of cryptocurrency before long. At least—as long as she stuck with him. The thought that she might not left a foul taste in his mouth and he stepped in front of her, stopping her in mid-step.

Confused, Erica looked up, and he spotted a hint of pizza sauce and cheese on her soft, full lips.

"You make me crazy," Brock said simply, and leaned down to kiss those small traces of her dinner away. He'd meant it as a simple tease, but the moment their lips brushed, the game ended.

He tossed the remainders of his pizza slice into a nearby trash can and slid his arms around Erica's slender waist, pulling her tightly into him and deepening the kiss. Her soft moan drove his hunger even higher and he tangled his fingers in her hair, sliding his tongue in between her sweet lips to meet hers.

"Soy sauce ..." she whispered, as he almost lifted her onto his hips to get closer. "Not so bad ..."

Groaning with delight and laughing simultaneously, Brock cupped her cheek and urged her into an extended dance, lips, tongues, and teeth melding with a passion that had been just below the surface between them for so long.

His hand slipped from her waist and reached back to palm her ass possessively, pulling her forward so there was no question at all about his desire for her. Erica gasped and rocked her hips into his, tipping her head so Brock could blaze a fiery trail along her jaw and throat.

"Home," she finally whispered, after uncounted time had

passed with her hands all over his back, his chest, his own backside, and his lips had devoured as much as humanly possible with the fabric still frustratingly between them. "Take me home, Brock. Then ... take me."

She didn't have to ask twice, but the walk to the car would have been a lot faster if their arms hadn't remained around each other and Brock hadn't kept stealing tastes of those gorgeous breasts, tracing their softest skin with his tongue wherever possible, feeling them arch up into him as Erica gave herself over willingly.

"So beautiful," he whispered when they were finally forced to separate at the door to the Lexus. He trailed a finger down her flushed cheek, to the swollen fullness of her lip.

It seemed that the pause gave Erica a moment to worry, because she finally asked the question Brock sensed she'd been wondering about for a while. "What happens after?"

"I don't know," he said honestly. "I'm not into commitment, Erica. I can give you tonight. And I can promise this won't affect the workplace at all. You have my word."

It was a lie, they both knew, but she seemed to accept it and nodded, leaning in for one more hungry kiss before Brock got into the car and pushed every speed limit back to her place.

CHAPTER 9

Erica could feel her heart pounding in her chest as she unlocked the door to the apartment and allowed Brock in. He walked inside and she took a second to appreciate the firm, muscular planes of his back and the tight curve of his ass before walking in and closing the door.

"Nice place," he said huskily, gesturing around. "Those are yours, I'm guessing?" As he spoke, he walked over to an abstract painting of the L. She'd told him tonight about her painting, and he'd listened carefully, it turned out, as he commented, "This is the one you said you painted after you and Joseph called it quits."

It was. She'd always painted as a hobby, going as far as having a few very small shows, but the breakup with her year-long boyfriend had triggered a painting spree, where Erica had repainted many of the places that had somehow been "theirs," finding her way back to a mentality where the places were generic and not quite so personal anymore.

"Yeah. Because that was the first place he ever kissed me, on the train," she explained, unaccountably nervous as Brock assessed her work.

"It's really good," he said quietly, and turned to look at her. The admiration she saw in his gaze, alongside the hunger, made Erica want him even more. "I'd like to kiss you on a train. Or anywhere else, for that matter. But kissing you right here is a good start." He crooked his finger and Erica took a slow breath and walked over, turning her back toward him as she did.

"I was wondering if you might give me a hand with getting the back of this dress unzipped," she murmured, casting a glance over her shoulder. "The last thing I want to do is tear it ..."

Brock's jaw dropped slightly. Then his eyes flashed and she saw him commit fully to the game. And that was exactly what this was, she decided, as he moved over to her, turning her around with light fingertips on her back that nevertheless made her skin almost burst into flames. They were playing a game, and she had no idea what the rules were. And fuck it, for once, she could not have cared less.

She turned around, and he unzipped the back of the garment, exposing her skin until she was covered in goosebumps. Then he leaned forward and buried his face in the back of her neck. Erica moaned.

He kissed her lightly, working his way up and down her neck, reaching around the front of her with his other hand as he did so, lightly cupping her breast in his hand. His big hand covered her completely, palming and kneading, lightly rolling her erect nipple until she was panting with need, before he finally snapped the clasp on her bra and let it fall away, replacing it once more with his hand, but this time skin on skin.

"Fuck," Erica moaned, letting her head fall back against his shoulder. "Just like that, Brock ..."

Instead, he turned her to face him and kissed her hard before pushing the fabric from her shoulders and staring down at her breasts with such overt hunger that a rush of heat flooded between Erica's legs, making her tremble.

"So fucking perfect," he growled, leaning down to rain kisses all over her neck, shoulders, and clavicle, until she thought she'd scream from need. As he did, she undressed him at a frantic pace, needing to have her own hands and lips on his perfect skin. Just as she pushed his shirt from his body, Brock finally lowered his mouth to her left breast and began a slow, hungry ravishing. His mouth was utter magic, working her nipple in a way that made Erica see stars.

She tangled her hands in his hair and let her head fall back, moaning unabashedly as Brock continued to devour her unhurriedly before suddenly sweeping her into his arms.

She gasped in total surprise, holding on tight as he bore her to the closest flat surface, which turned out to be the couch.

Sprawling out on it with her on top of him, Brock drew her into a heated kiss as his hands moved over her body, sliding between her legs to stroke her soaking heat, filling her first with one finger, than another.

"Ride my fingers, baby," he murmured, as he lifted her higher to kiss the undersides of each breast, trailing towards her stomach with every searing touch.

She did, grinding down, her gasps turning into moans, which turned into cries of pleasure as, just with his fingers, he seemed to reach deeper than any other man ever had.

"Are you going to come just like that?" Brock asked, using his free hand to squeeze her ass firmly, making Erica shudder even more.

"God ... yes ..." she cried, eyes almost rolling back in her head as he rocked the heel of his hand against her clit.

"I want to see you," he urged, and the look of rapt desire on his face send Erica over the edge, crying out with pleasure over and over until she sagged forward over him, coming to rest on his perfect chest.

"I'm going to watch that happen several times again tonight," Brock murmured in her ear after she'd come down slightly from her high, his hands still roaming over her, this time from shoulder to ass and then back up once more. She shivered pleasurably when he playfully spanked her just slightly, and he chuckled.

"If you like that, there's plenty more, baby."

She could feel him beneath her, his heavy cock still in his pants, straining to break free. "I get a turn first," Erica murmured, sitting back and kissing him slowly as the fall of her hair created a curtain around them for a long minute before she climbed off the couch and took Brock's hand.

Somehow, they found their way to the bedroom, kissing every other footstep. When they got there, Erica guided him to sit and then knelt before him.

"Fuck," Brock whispered, before she'd even touched him, and she smile as she reached for the zipper of his pants, easing it open and then shoving his pants and briefs down. He sprang free, every bit as large and thick as he'd felt when she'd been lying over him.

Erica licked her lips in anticipation and pressed a teasing kiss just to the head. Brock's dark groan almost killed her initial plan to go slow, but she managed to hold onto a thread of her original intent, teasing him in slow stages by curling her tongue around him, pumping him firmly with his hand while she kissed his slit and lightly cupped his balls, rolling them in her hand. Then, as his breathing grew labored and his cursing grew louder, she parted her lips and drew her into her mouth.

"Shit! Erica!" Brock cried out, which only encouraged her further as she took him deeper, feeling her cheeks stretch with his width as she gradually worked her way all the way down to his base.

When she had him all the way in and he was cursing a heady blue streak, she drew back and took him completely in again, then again, alternating sucking with deepthroating, humming softly to add to his pleasure.

Brock shuddered and bucked under her, lacing his fingers through her hair and guiding her movements lightly, whispering garbled words of need that mostly came out "Fuck ... fuck ... fuck ... so fuckin' hot ... so fuckin' tight ..."

She reveled in the combination of her power over him and the way he dominated her with his hands occasionally, forcing her to take him deeper when he got frantic.

As she felt his balls draw up and begin to tighten, she drew back, letting his cock go with a wet, regretful pop.

"Next time you can come in my mouth," she promised, standing on shaky knees to kiss him hard. "Right now, I want you inside me, though."

She didn't have to ask twice.

"Get on your hands and knees," Brock rasped, and Erica hurried to do so, shuddering as she felt him climb up behind her on the bed, felt his big body position itself around hers, and then felt the huge head of his cock nudge against her sex.

She groaned at the feeling, then yelped as his palm descended on her ass, slapping her firmly. "You want this, baby?"

"Yes!" she cried out, and he spanked her again.

"How bad? Tell me."

His palm descended again, making contact lightly but firmly, massaging, retreating, then descending once more as Erica cried out in incoherent pleasure, pleading for him.

When it appeared she'd satisfied Brock with her desire, the spanking stopped and he spread her legs. In one hard thrust, he sheathed himself within her and Erica screamed this time, jolting forward under the force of being impaled on his huge cock.

"YES!"

"Perfect," he groaned, setting up a brutal pounding rhythm, raining soft bites all over her neck and shoulders as he took her hard. "You're so tight around me, Erica. You're taking all of me, baby, and you're still so tight ... fuck ... yessssss ..."

He built their pleasure higher and higher, until Erica's throat was nearly hoarse from screaming her need. Then, as she felt his thrusts begin to get ragged, he reached around and rubbed her clit, hard, and she came apart beneath him, crying out his name in the most violent orgasm she'd had in her life.

He was right behind her in more ways than one, groaning her name as he spilled deep, deep inside her.

They lay still like that for a long, endless moment, while Erica's sight finally returned after she'd been completely blinded by pleasure.

And then Brock's mouth was at her ear again, and he was whispering, "You're amazing," before slowly withdrawing and collapsing onto the bed just as Erica did, rolling onto her back to get her breath.

Then they lay there in quiet silence that rapidly grew awkward.

And that's that ... Erica thought as Brock rolled out of bed abruptly.

"Sorry, I've got to grab a few things in the morning for work, so it's going to be a lot better if I just sleep there. I hope that's okay?"

Erica nodded, masking her disappointment. "Of course. See you tomorrow."

And all at once, he was gone. Erica sighed. She didn't know how she felt at that moment, and wondered if it was how all women felt after they had sex. She wasn't a virgin, but it was the first time in her life she had had an orgasm. In fact, he had given her two orgasms by the time he had finished, and she felt more satisfied than she had ever felt in her entire life.

But she had to force herself not to think of what Meagan had said to her the other day. She had told her that it was perfectly fine that she was taking the money because she wasn't sleeping with him—and now she was.

Or was she? Was this a one-time thing, or were they going to start having sex with each other regularly? She didn't want to get in over her head, but she also didn't want to do anything that would jeopardize her position at work, or her reputation in the world.

There were so many thoughts and emotions running through her mind, and she didn't know which ones she should follow. She had had sex with her boss, and she was flat out falling for him too. No amount of denial was going to change either fact, and she was going to have to get up and go to work the next day, trying to function as she always did without bringing up what they had just done tonight.

But then she thought about what they had just done—and how badly she wanted to do it again.

CHAPTER 10

Brock didn't know what had happened to him, but he couldn't get Erica off his mind. The night after they had sex he had gone home and slept. Finally, he had slept. And he had woken up feeling refreshed. He couldn't believe he had finally had sex with the woman he had been yearning for for so long, and it felt good.

Part of him was worried that she was going to regret what she had done when she woke. He grabbed his phone, worried that there was already a message on it saying that she wasn't happy about the night before, or that she wanted to speak with him.

But his phone only held messages that were about work, and he dismissed them all.

He got up and showered, thinking about everything they had done the night before. It didn't matter what he did, Erica was on the front of his mind, consuming every single spare thought that he had, and he was glad. For the first time ever, he regretted leaving a woman's bed and apartment. But he couldn't have stayed, obviously. This wasn't a relationship. He wasn't sure if it was a one-night stand, or one that would turn into several, but it still was no girlfriend, boyfriend thing. He didn't play that game, and he'd been clear about his lack of interest in commitment.

Once he got out of the shower, he walked back over to the bed. At the back of his mind, he knew that it would be the right thing to do to send her a text. It had been a great evening, even beyond the sex. A nice guy sent something the night after. But when he pulled up his phone, his mind went blank.

Finally, he just sent, Thinking of you. After he sent it, he second-guessed himself, which Brock rarely did, and continued to do so as he got dressed and started the drive to work. There were too many ways the message could be misread. It sounded deeper and more intimate than he'd intended. But it also seemed shallow, not even mentioning the particulars of the night.

All the way to work, Brock thought about her, and even wondered what her eyes would be like when they woke and were hazy with sleep. Just wondering that scared the crap out of him, because one thing Brock didn't do was morning-after scenes. Never had. Never intended to. Waaaay too intimate.

Commitment scared him. He'd seen how his parents had torn each other to pieces, and he wanted no part of that pie. So how to let Erica know that she was special, and last night had also been, without letting on how much she'd rocked him completely, therefore giving her ideas and making himself vulnerable? There had to be a way. Brock excelled at blazing paths where there were none to be found.

It was a long, awkward morning, with Erica obviously avoiding him. It bothered Brock more than he cared to admit that she was clearly hurt, and that he missed their easy interactions. Finally, Brock couldn't put it off any longer and sent her a text, even though she was just one room away.

Got a second?

A moment later, there was a knock on the door and he drew a slow breath before calling, "Come on in."

She walked in, her eyes looking every which way, far from the confident person he'd come to know. Even as he took in her pallor and nervousness, he couldn't help but notice how good she looked. It seemed that she just didn't have a bad day in her; she was beautiful morning, noon, and night.

"Can I help you with something?" she finally said, hovering in front of his desk until he waved her into a chair. "Run an errand? Reschedule a—"

"It's not work-related," Brock cut in, opting for blunt, since that was his comfort zone. "Are you okay, Erica?"

She gave him a look. "Not exactly. You know why. But I knew it would affect work, so it's on me."

He winced. "No, it's just as much on me." Then he didn't know what else to say. Sorry? But he wasn't. Not at all. And he'd told her what to expect, right?

There was an awkward pause between them, and Brock felt his thoughts racing. He didn't know what had come over him. With the rest of the world, he was the suave and smooth businessman, able to handle and take care of anything. It was often said that no one and nothing could rattle him, and it was a rumor that he had often lived up to with pride.

But with this girl seated on the chair on the opposite side of his desk, he couldn't help but feel nervous. For the first time in his life, he wasn't nervous about what she was going to say when she left, he was worried that he was going to say something that would make her leave. She hadn't said anything about the text that he had sent her that morning, and that fact in itself bothered him.

"If that's all, then I'll get back to work." Erica got to her feet abruptly. "I'll deal with it, Brock. I'm a grown woman. I made a choice last night. I don't regret it, even if this is the result."

Somehow, hearing that she didn't regret it eased some of Brock's own tension. He got to his feet and moved in front of Erica, to cut her off from the door.

She gave him a warning look. "I have work to do, Brock. Your work."

The hurt in her eyes shattered what was left his walls and he reached out and hauled her into him, kissing her fiercely.

For one brief second, Erica resisted, but then she melted into him and he groaned with relief, plunging between her soft lips. "I'm sorry I'm such a shit," he whispered, smoothing her hair back and trailing his hands down her lush body.

"Don't talk," she whispered, swiftly unbuttoning the front of his shirt and scattering kisses over his chest. "Just do, Brock. Before my brain full engages."

Somehow, he broke away from her long enough to lock the door. When he turned back, she was standing by his desk, her shirt halfway off, just like his. Brock caught her lips again and ravaged them, before slipping the remainder of her clothing off and just taking a step to revel in the goddess who was now fully naked in his office.

"Fuck, you're the most beautiful creature on earth," he groaned, going to his knees and hooking Erica's hips with one arm. He pulled her into him and set his mouth between her legs, feasting on the hot, melting warmth. Her muffled groans only spurred him onward to hold her legs wider open, tracing his tongue up and down her lips, nibbling at them, suckling, before plunging two fingers deep inside at the same time that he kissed her clit.

The way Erica bucked and writhed made it almost impossible to stop, and her breathy little gasps pushed him right to the brink himself, but finally he managed to pull away before he undid them both completely. They'd only have one time before someone or other interrupted them, so he wanted them both to come together.

Kissing his way back up her lovely body, lingering at the soft rise of her stomach and moving into the full swells of her breasts, Brock devoured each breast in slow turn before turning Erica to face the desk.

"I've fantasized about this constantly," she whispered as he undid his pants, pulling out his rigid cock.

"Did you use just your fingers?" he whispered back, leaning into her ear as he slowly pushed himself deep inside, shuddering at how tight and wet she was. "Fuck, baby. Ahhh ... fuck ... yes."

"No. Vibrator," she gasped, as Brock reached around to stroke her clit in time with each thrust. "Brock ... oh God ... I'm already so close ..."

Imagining her in bed with her legs splayed, her toy working between her beautiful pale thighs, making her shudder and scream in ecstasy, drove Brock half insane. He thrust into her wildly, and when she started to get too loud, he reached for his tie and stuffed it into her mouth, which seemed to make her even crazier.

She bucked against him, breath ragged, breasts heaving, her moans and whimpers resonating at the very core of his own body.

"Erica ... Erica ..." he growled over and over, biting her shoulder lightly as her felt her start to come, and the tightening around his cock triggered his own explosive orgasm, so violent that if the desk hadn't been so strong, it would've been shaking.

He held her to him as he emptied himself deep inside, whispering raw nothings that he was glad nobody could possibly have understood, because they came from the softest part of him, his heart, where he never let anybody in.

Finally, Brock slipped out of Erica and turned her back to face him.

The dazed look on her face very nearly made him hard again and he leaned down to kiss her, letting her taste herself on his lips.

"Beautiful," he whispered, brushing a tender kiss on each breast before slowly stepping back. "I hate to let you go." As he spoke, he realized he meant it more ways than one.

"Damn meetings," Erica laughed breathlessly, beginning to collect her clothes. Brock didn't make it easy on her, he admitted to himself later, interrupting her at every turn with another kiss, pressing his lips to each sweet, tender spot before it vanished beneath the unwanted fabric, until her blouse was finally fully buttoned and she somehow managed to pat her hair back into place.

"One sec," Brock said, before she stepped out of the office. He picked up the phone. "Hey, Ange, do me a favor? There's a package that was supposed to be delivered today and I haven't seen it. Erica's out on some kind of errand. Can you check? Thanks."

A moment later, he hung up and smiled at Erica. "Coast is clear."

As she smiled back and slipped out of the office, Brock stood there, frozen, staring after her, the realization sinking in more than ever.

He was crazy about her.

Damn it all.

CHAPTER 11

"I know, I know, I know." Erica fended off Meagan's scolding, hunching over the salad she'd been trying to eat ever since they got to their usual favorite lunch spot. She'd made the mistake of telling Meagan everything and was now paying dearly for it.

"You realize this is exactly what he wanted," Meagan went on. "Paying off your debts was just an opener. He probably hired you because he liked how you look—"

"Stop!" Erica cut in, finally having had enough, and Meagan must have heard the edge in her tone because she finally shut up. "I get it. I fell for my boss—yes, I fell for him, it wasn't just me climbing into bed with nobody—" she said in response to her best friend's suddenly wide eyes, "I fell for him, and that was my first mistake. My second was taking the money, and my third was sleeping with him. But he hired me because of my talent, Meagan. You said from the very beginning that it would be about my looks and that was insulting then. It's insulting now." Throwing down a few bills, Erica stood up, giving up on lunch.

"Wait," Meagan said hastily, getting up too and reaching out a hand. "Erica, I didn't mean it that way. I just don't want you to get hurt."

Erica stood stiffly, hating the tears in her eyes. "It's not like I think it'll work between us. How could it? He's a billionaire and I'm some college student off the street who happened to get lucky enough to be hired by him. He's a playboy. He's been completely upfront about that. He doesn't want to commit. I get it. I'm fully aware of the fucking reality. But that doesn't make a bit of difference in how I feel." She grabbed a napkin, jabbed at her eyes with it, and walked away.

As she did, with Meagan hurrying alongside her desperately, Erica's phone started buzzing, and she looked down at it. "I don't know who this is," she muttered, stepping outside of the café and answering. "Hello?"

"Yes, is this Miss Samson?" She didn't recognize the voice on the other end of the line.

"Yes?" Erica said uncertainly, shrugging her shoulders at Meagan's quizzical look.

"This is Officer Johnson. Ma'am, your father has just been transported to the hospital."

Erica's heart froze and she momentarily blanked out everything else the officer was saying until she finally registered the words heart attack heart attack heart attack, and they rattled around in her brain until they forced words from her lips.

"Oh my God. Is he going to be okay?" she cried into the phone, leaning into Meagan's immediately supportive arm. "Where did you say he is? Is he going to be okay?"

"Ma'am, all I can tell you is that he is at the hospital right now." The officer rattled off a name and address and then hung up, shaking violently.

"I'll drive," Meagan said firmly, having gathered the gist of the conversation from Erica's reaction. As she guided Erica along the street, the world seemed hazy and out of focus.

She couldn't bring herself to think of something bad happening to her father. She'd barely known her mother. Her father had raised her by himself and was the best man she knew.

"He has to be okay," she whispered, tears streaming down her face as Meagan ushered her into her car and then sped toward the hospital.

THE NEXT 48 hours were a living nightmare. From the moment they arrived in the hospital until Monday afternoon, when yet another heart specialist arrived to speak with her, all Erica could do was sit helplessly by her father's bedside, where he was surrounded by so much machinery that it felt like a factory. There were so many tubes in his work-worn hands that she couldn't even hold one, so she settled for staying awake beside him, touching his shoulder frequently, whispering prayers and pleas.

The specialist rambled on about her father's heart condition, the reason for the induced coma, all the things Erica had been hearing for days, and then threw one more iron in the fire.

"He'll require further surgery. His heart is so badly scarred from previous trauma that we weren't able to fully perform the necessary procedures the first time."

Erica had barely recovered from hearing that, when the surgeon continued, "We don't think he'll need to be put on a transplant list, but he'll require intensive care for quite some time, to get him back to health. And after that, he'll need to see …"

Erica heard the long list of specialist and therapists and medications, even as she knew they didn't have the money to pay for it. Her father's pre-existing conditions had been the death sentence on any number of insurance plans they'd applied for over the years.

She managed to somehow thank the doctor and saw him to the door, then was sinking back into her chair when a familiar voice made her head shoot up.

"How is he?"

"Brock," she exclaimed in surprise, jumping back up to her feet and realizing that in the chaos, she'd completely forgotten to call work. She'd simply skipped going in. "Oh my god, I'm so—"

Then he was beside her, drawing her into his arms, holding her tight. "Shh. How is he?" he repeated, and Erica broke down and cried for the hundredth time, leaning into Brock's big, broad chest as he kissed her hair and whispered soft, reassuring words.

Finally, she drew back and managed to sniff, "How did you know?"

"Your best friend called," he replied, snagging a tissue from a nearby box and gently wiping her face. "You should've called. I would've been here immediately, Erica."

"I wasn't thinking about anything except him." She looked at her still, silent father and tears overflowed her eyes again. "He can't die. He just can't. It sounds so selfish, but I'll be all alone." Her voice cracked.

Brock slid an arm around her waist. "You're not alone, sweetheart. I know I told you I'm not into commitment, and I'm not. But that doesn't mean I won't be here for you."

His words felt bizarrely discordant with his sudden appearance and she went from feeling reassured and supported, to alone all over again. It was like he just had to drive home that one point.

"I don't even know what that means." Erica drew away and folded her arms around herself, desperately cold in this lonely, sterile room. "What exactly are we, if we're not committed?"

He grimaced and she kicked herself around the block, already knowing the next words out of his mouth. "I told you before ... everything. I just don't do that kind of stuff. I'm your friend, Erica. Your boss. Your friend. Your lover sometimes."

She clenched her jaw so tightly it hurt. "Of course. You did tell me. I'm the one who deluded myself into thinking I could possibly be more."

She needed to walk. She'd been cooped up into this room for too long. Needing air, she started for the door and headed down the hallway, not knowing where she was going, but unable to stop moving.

Brock kept pace with her easily. "Erica. I know it sounds terrible, but it's honestly not you. I swear, the problem is all—"

"Oh, I know where the problem is," she interrupted, taking the stairs two at a time. "And I'm no innocent. You were upfront, and I should've seen it coming. I let myself be bought almost from day one. My salary. My debts."

"Whoa!" Brock protested, as she nearly slammed the door to the lobby in his face, still keeping close on her heels. "Yes, you looked drop-dead gorgeous when I hired you, but I don't hire employees because of knockout legs and breasts that keep me hard 24/7. Damn it, Erica, I hired you because of your brain. Would you stop for just one second?!"

She had stopped, finally, and was staring at a magazine in the hospital's giftshop. Reaching out, Erica picked it up and stared at the cover. Brock glanced at it and groaned. "Erica—"

It was a standard tabloid, supermarket style, filled with celebrities and diet tricks. And on the cover was her boss, her lover, her "friend" passionately making out with a certain celeb du jour.

"That wasn't recent," Brock began, and Erica waved him away, putting the magazine back down and resuming her endless walk.

"You don't have to apologize. Like you said. We're nothing. And even if we were something, which we'll never be, I know, I know, that doesn't matter right now. What does is that my father may be dying. That is all that matters to me, Brock. You are no longer important. Maybe you've never heard those words before, so hear them clearly from me."

She pivoted and faced him dead on, not even angry as she looked into his handsome, shocked faced. All she felt was empty. Hollowed out. "You are no longer important. I would like to keep my job, because I have to once again pay my bills along with my father's, but that is the only reason I don't outright quit. Please don't fire me. If I have to beg, I will. For him. Not for me."

He blanched, but she didn't have enough energy left in her to regret her words. "I would never fire you. Erica, I'll pay for his care so you don't have to worry—"

"Not on your life." She drew herself up to her slight height. "I can take out loans. I will take out loans. I cared for him before, and I will care for him again. You're not buying me a second time. Maybe it would be best for Dad. Probably it would be. But he'd die for sure if he knew I let you give me one more penny. Thank you, but no thank you. So long as you'll still have me as an employee, I'll see you at work in a couple days. I'll need a few days of leave to finish figuring things out here."

Brock stared at her for a long, endless moment before silently nodding.

Nodding back, Erica exhaled a long, slow breath and walked away. This time he didn't follow her.

CHAPTER 12

"I told her exactly what the deal was," Brock muttered, downing another shot beside Jack at the bar. "Just like with every other woman, I was crystal clear on the deal."

UNUSUALLY PATIENTLY, Jack sat and drank, just listening.

"She acted like I'd promised her ... I don't know ... marriage, or something," Brock exclaimed, waving at the bartender for another round. "What the fuck!"

Jack continued to sit quietly and Brock finally exploded. "What? Say something!"

"You won't like it."

Brock's eyebrows hit the ceiling. "When have you ever told me what I want to hear? That's not how this relationship works."

"Oh, so you're committed to at least one relationship, then?" Jack said dryly.

"What is that—"

"It means that you're a good guy, Brock, and you're my best friend, but you're one hell of a selfish son of a bitch." Jack shook his head and took a slow sip of something or other that wasn't a shot. What the hell had he been drinking while Brock had been downing drink after drink?

"Meaning?" Brock snapped.

"Meaning that her father could be dead as we speak and you're making this entirely about you. You walked into that hospital room and some of the first words out of your mouth weren't 'I'm so sorry, baby. What can I do?' No, you had to make sure she was crystal clear on your commitment issues first."

Brock stopped in mid-shot, his anger slowly fading. "I didn't even tell you what I said."

Jack snorted. "You didn't need to. I know you, man. I've known you. I'll continue to know you. And selfish is all well and good. I'm fuckin' selfish myself. But even I know better than to do what you undoubtedly did. And you did. Didn't you."

Brock looked down at his shot glass, thinking of his words to her.

You're not alone, sweetheart. I know I told you I'm not into commitment, and I'm not. But that doesn't mean I won't be here for you.

"I did," he admitted gruffly, having a hard time believing it in hindsight. "I was just so panicked. Meagan called me and I dropped everything and ran to be with Erica. And then I got there and she looked so small and broken, Jack. Damn it." He slammed a fist on the bar and waved the bartender's questioning glare away. "All I wanted to do was hold her tight and promise her to fix things. I've never felt that way before. Ever."

"And it scared the shit out of you." Jack nodded, clapping a hand on Brock's shoulder and getting to his feet. "I don't want to leave you to drink alone, but I have a date."

It felt like the entire world as Brock had known it was imploding from the edges. "You? A date?" He stared at his best friend, who'd never said the single-syllable word before without making it sound like a substantial curse.

"With Angie," Jack said sympathetically, shoving a few bills in front of Brock to take care of his tab.

"Angie?"

"You broke her heart too. Who knows. I might do the same. But I'm going to go try not to tonight, anyway. Night, man."

Jack walked away, leaving Brock gaping after him through the bar's thick, smoky haze.

He wasn't sure how long he sat there before a long-legged beauty with eyes like hot, hungry coals, and breasts so full it was a miracle her shirt didn't pop, sidled onto the stool beside his.

"Hey, handsome."

Brock barely gave her a glance. "Hi."

"You look like you could use a dance," she offered, waving at a corner of the room where some people had created an impromptu dance floor.

He shook his head. "No. Sorry. Really not interested."

Apparently as unused to be turned down as Brock himself was, the woman persisted. "I'm Naomi. Love troubles, I'm guessing?"

Brock rolled his eyes. "Not even close. That would involve love, and I have no love in my life."

As he spoke the words and saw the sympathy cross Naomi's face, he realized what he'd said. And it was true. He had no love in his life. No family. No friends besides Jack, who most days was hit or miss. Not even any real acquaintances outside of work. What he had was an endless list of women he could contact at a moment's notice for a one-night stand. He had women, yeah. And work. Plenty of that. And money. Tons of it. So much he didn't know what to do with it.

Except ... he did it.

"You're right." Brock nodded and got up, gesturing at the

bartender. "Buy the lady as many drinks as she wants. Any her friends might want, too. Put it on my tab."

Naomi frowned, defeat sitting poorly on her pretty features. "Where are you going?"

"To show some love with the only thing I have a whole lot of."

CHAPTER 13

Three Months Later

"See to it that you get it done!"

"Yes, Mr. Cornwall." Erica sighed as she walked back to the kitchen, her arms loaded down with a tray full of dirty dishes. As she bumped open the door with her hip, the heavy, humid stench of a 24-hour diner in full swing hit her hard.

She made her way to the back to drop off the dishes, and as she walked, she tuned out the ache of her back and neck and arms and feet as she often did, by replaying the final moments before she'd walked out of Brock's life forever.

It felt trite and melodramatic now, but at the time she'd felt she had to take a stand when she'd discovered that he'd gone ahead and pried into her father's affairs, somehow illegally finding out what medical treatment he needed, then paying for it. Even after she'd specifically told him not to do it, he had, and that had been the last straw. She'd told him so at the office, in front of half the eavesdropping staff, watching the stunned look cross his face before she'd walked out and never gone back.

"I wouldn't mind a billionaire of my own," Gabby, her only

friend at the diner, quipped as she and Erica crossed paths, she on the way to the kitchen, Erica on her way back to the main floor. "At this time of my night, my feet start screaming for money as much as mercy."

Erica gave her a rueful smile and went about her job efficiently, bussing tables even though she was ostensibly a waitress. With no waitressing experience under her belt, the only way Cornwall had hired her had been when she swore to do anything at all. Brock had paid for her father's bills, and there had been nothing Erica could do to change that. Frankly, it would have been stupid to try, after the fact. Her father was getting the best possible care and even then, there were days when he was doing well, then there were days when he was back at death's door. Every time she thought that he was going to pull through and be able to go home with her, something would happen and his health would take a turn for the worse once more. It seemed like a never-ending nightmare that she could never wake up from.

But though Brock had paid for all the bills he'd assumed would come with treatment, he hadn't realized the extent of the care. Those were the bills Erica now labored to pay off. She'd started by selling her car and now caught the bus to work. Regular night shifts, and she just barely managed to keep a roof on her head and the extra medical bills up to date. Food was a hit or miss, but she rarely wanted any after scraping people's leftovers all day. That had been Cornwall's deal. He'd hire her, and he'd pay her marginally better than minimum wage, but she would do anything from scrubbing toilets to waitressing. And she did.

A group of rowdy customers walked in and Erica rushed to wash her hands before going to attend to them. "Gentlemen," she greeted them as cheerfully as she was able. "What can I get started for you this evening? Some coffee?"

The largest man in the group, a good 300 pounds, at the very least, gave her a slow once over and Erica groaned inwardly, knowing exactly how this was going to go. "I know what I want to get started, sweet cheeks."

Keeping her smile grimly in place, Erica repeated, "Coffee? I just made a pot. Why don't I go ahead and bring you all some."

"That's not the some I want," Lardo drawled, eyes lingering on her breasts.

"That something is taken," she replied with as much false warmth as she could muster, and waving her hand with its fake wedding band. Sometimes that did the trick.

Lardo laughed uproariously and slapped his friend on the back, almost sending him straight into the sugar stand. "Bring us coffee, sugar tits."

Swallowing a sigh of relief, Erica turned to go, only to feel a hard, firm squeeze on her left cheek. It was all she could do not to scream, but she needed this job. Between this night shift and a temp position doing data entry, she was making it. It wouldn't always be like this, she vowed to herself, as she poured four cups of coffee with shaking hands and fought the urge to poison them with the toilet cleaner she'd been using earlier. She had interviews. Seemed like next to nobody was hiring, but she at least had interviews.

One day, I'll get on my feet, she promised herself, scrubbing at her eyes with her sleeve before returning to her only customers for the evening. If she was extra nice to them, they might even leave a nice tip.

"Here you go. Fresh, hot coffee," she chirped, placing a mug in front of each burly man.

"I'm pretty hot, baby," a guy with a bad case of cystic acne, somewhat covered by a scraggly beard, informed her. "Want to feel how hot?"

"Married," she said again, waving her hand once more. "My

husband gets awfully jealous and you boys wouldn't want me to get in trouble at home, I'm sure. Now. What sounds good for dinner?"

There was a jingle behind Erica and she called out, "I'll be with you in just a minute. Have a seat anywhere you'd like," before looking at her customers.

"I'd like to eat you," Acne informed her, his eyes directed to the apex of her thighs.

She clenched her hand around her pen, praying for control of her temper. "Our blue plate special is blackened catfish and a side of jambalaya. I highly recommend it."

"How much for a taste?" Lardo pressed, darting a meaty hand out for another hungry squeeze.

"Honey, I am way too expensive for you," Erica said sweetly, praying that her slip of the tongue didn't elicit a tantrum.

Instead, he seemed to not even hear it, so intent was he on feeling her up no matter where she stood. And if she moved to the left, Acne was there. If she moved a little further, the silent men she'd dubbed Red Nose and Yellow Teeth, took their turns.

At her wits' end, she heard the jingle again and turned, not seeing anyone. Apparently her other customer had been uninterested in waiting around. Erica glanced at the clock 5:45 a.m. She just had to make it till 6:30.

Pasting a sickening grin on her face, one she felt all the way to her gut, she refocused on her table and on trying to get some kind of a dinner or breakfast order out of them, without stabbing them all with the surprisingly sharp butter knives.

CHAPTER 14

Brock racked the last weight and headed for the shower, every muscle in his body aching. As he scrubbed off, he ran over his mile-long list for the afternoon. The new personal assistant he'd hired was a competent kid and kept him on track most of the time, but some days even Adam couldn't keep up with Brock's jampacked schedule.

Ever since losing Erica—because he'd long ago realized that that was exactly what her departure had been, a total loss for him in more ways than one—he'd buried himself up to his neck in more work than he'd seen since he first started the business. The only time he gave himself a break was at lunch, where he allowed for 20 minutes or so to eat, and a full hour to workout. It was the only thing that was keeping him marginally sane, even if he came in at 7:00 a.m. or stayed till 10:00 p.m. to compensate for that time.

He'd designed the gym so it had actual closets instead of just lockers, and one of those closets, his own personal one, held fresh suits, one which he now donned before starting toward the elevator and the office once more. As he walked, Erica's face floated before him and he firmly put it aside. For weeks, he'd been furious at her for humiliating in front of his whole office for doing something nice. Something he thought he'd done out of love, until Brock had finally realized that Jack had been right all along. Bribing people to get information about Noel Samson's necessities had really been more about assuaging his own guilt at his behavior. He'd brought Erica on, seduced her—even if there had been two to that tango, he knew very well who had been the more experienced and manipulative of the two of them—and then broken her heart at a time when she'd needed her whole focus to be on her father. Then he'd done it a second time, trying to buy his way out of relationship prison, and she'd called time on him so fast that his head was still spinning.

He missed her, Brock reflected as he walked into the office, straightening his tie. Missed seeing at her desk. Missed seeing her in the conference room and the hallways. Missed watching her walk by his office, totally focused on some errand or other—

"Earth to Brock."

He jolted back to reality, seeing Angie standing before him with an exasperated expression that suggested she'd been trying to get his attention for a while.

"Sorry. What's up?"

She nodded at his office. "Can we talk in private?"

Surprised, Brock nodded. "Sure. Come on in." He held the door and followed behind Angie as she walked inside.

He closed the door and started to take a seat when she stopped him, holding out an envelope. Confused, Brock took it and stared down at the printed label.

Angela Varvatos

Letter of Resignation

"Angie," he said in shock, looking back up at her. "What—why—okay, I didn't see this coming."

"You haven't seen anything coming since Erica left," Angie informed him wryly. "You're lost, Brock. Own it."

"Oh, I do," he muttered, dragging a hand through his hair as he looked at the envelope once more. "Believe me, I am fully aware that my path got lost three months back. Why, Angie?"

"Why are you lost, or why am I quitting?" She didn't give him a chance to answer. "I was a total bitch to Erica. Did you even notice that?"

"No," he admitted. "I didn't."

She nodded. "You're the best at your business, but you suck at human relationships, Brock. I'm really not much better, which is one of the reasons I'm leaving. Life is too short to be playing the jealous games I'm good at. There's gotta be more."

"Jealous?"

She rolled her eyes. "Duh. I wanted to hand this personally to you for two reasons. One, because you were a good boss. A bastard of a guy, but unintentionally for the most part, I think. And two, because I might be able to help you out."

"Help me out with what?" he asked tersely, getting tired of being put in his place so often by so many, so recently. He'd already admitted his mistakes. The world could now stop throwing them back in his face, thank you very much.

"I bumped into Erica last week."

Brock turned from his desk, where he'd been about to walk over to. "What?" Something inside him that had been dead for months roared to life, and it wasn't his libido. Not entirely, anyway.

"I saw her accidentally, and I've been debating ever since whether I should let you know," Angie replied.

Brock was over at her side in two seconds flat, his hands on her shoulders. "Angie. Where is she? I have to know. She won't answer my emails or my texts. Her landlord has no idea where she went. All my money won't get me answers about where she's staying, even when I have an idea of what facility her father is being treated at."

"And you really, really want to know, huh," Angie mocked him slightly. "Because the girl stole your heart from the minute she walked into this office. I'll tell you, but on one condition only."

"What?" he said desperately. "Anything. You want a nice severance check, even though you're not being fired? Done."

"I wouldn't mind that," she said with a laugh, "but you've got to quit with throwing money at people who care about you. We'll still care, even if you don't shove cash our direction, Brock." For the first time in his memory, Angie's eyes were soft, instead of hard as flint. "And I do care about you, even if you're so lost in your misery that you don't even notice this."

She lifted her hand, displaying a prominent engagement ring.

For a moment, Brock just stared at it, before look back at Angie's face. "Jack proposed?"

She nodded. "Maybe I'm going to end up with him where I did with you. Maybe not. But I'm going to take the risk that I won't. Say it, Brock." It was her turn to put her hand on his shoulder, as he tried to come to terms with how he'd tuned the world out so completely that even his best friend's very serious relationship had escaped him. "Just say the words about Erica, and I'll tell you where she is."

"I love her," he blurted out, the words that he'd so feared, for so long, falling out so naturally that when they did, they seemed to hang in mid-air. "Angie, I fucking love the woman. I need her like I need to breathe, dammit. I broke her heart, and then she carved my own out with a fucking spoon."

Angie smiled. "Think you can tell her that without all the four-letter embellishments? Girls think it's more romantic without. Just sayin'."

"Yes! Tell me!"

When she did, Brock lingered only long enough to hug her

hard, apologized for being a total ass time and time again, and then booked it out of the office, calling out to Adam as he ran past, "Cancel everything for today."

He had an appointment that mattered more than anything else on the agenda. In fact, he had a totally new agenda. It involved telling the woman of his dreams that she was his everything.

CHAPTER 15

"Erica..."

She sighed and looked up from the pan she was scouring to a shine, seeing the sympathy etched on Gabby's face. "I don't think I want to know."

"Lardo's back. Alone this time. And he's asking specifically for you."

"Shit," Erica yelled, dropping the clean pan back into the sink with a loud clang. "He's been here six days in a row. I'm going to run him through, Gabs. I swear."

"Murdering customers is inadvisable," Cornwall said dryly, and Erica jumped and spun, not having realized her boss was in the kitchen.

"Sir! I'm sorry," she stammered, blushing to the roots of her hair.

"Just get out there and show that man as a good a time as is legally possible," her boss ordered, stalking away to harangue the chef about something or other.

"You said you have an interview this Friday, right?" Gabby said, as Erica fought the urge to scream and simultaneously cry.

"Yeah. This is the last one at the accounting firm. I don't know why they'd have any interest in me, with no practical experience, but I guess the internships and the few months at Brock's office count for something." Saying his name hurt as always, but Erica didn't let it stop her. She scrubbed her hands clean, put a clean uniform blouse on, from the stash she kept in the breakroom—not that she ever got a break—and headed out to do battle.

Lardo's enormous face split into a huge grin as she walked over to him and stood with her pen poised over her pad, keeping as much of a distance as possible between them.

"Ain't you going to say hello, sugar tits?"

She gritted her teeth. "Hello, sugar tits." His tits were definitely way bigger than hers.

Lardo laughed so hard his fat rolls jiggled. "You're so feisty. I betcha you'll taste better than those pancakes you keep making me order so I can stay here night after night."

"More of the same?" she asked tersely.

"How about a kiss?" he countered. "Just one little peck ... maybe on the pecker ..."

Erica broke. Without a word, she turned, grabbed the remains of a pot of coffee on another table, one which she knew had been cooling for at least 20 minutes, and upended it over Lardo so abruptly that it took him a second to process the lukewarm fluid dousing him from head to crotch.

"Put your pecker in that, you sick, disgusting excuse for a human being," she snarled as he started to howl in rage. "I quit!"

She walked straight out the diner door and stood there for a second, fists clenched, breathing in the cold night air before turning in the direction of the bus station. As she did, she saw him.

Brock stood a few feet away, his suit so crisply pressed that

Erica briefly wondered if it was 9:00 a.m. instead of 4:00 a.m. He looked exactly like he had the day she left the office, with several additional pounds of muscle added to his frame, and a slightly shorter haircut, both with only served to make him even more masculine. The man was sex on legs, damn it.

"Why are you here?" she cried, trying not to stare into his incredible eyes or notice how soft the slight smile on his lips was. "How did you find me?"

"I watched that whole scene go down," Brock said quietly, not making a move toward her. "Just stood here and watched through the window as that fat ass put you through hell."

She blinked, her temper cooling abruptly, mostly due to a bucket of confusion that doused it. "You did?"

"Yeah. One of the hardest things I've ever done was not intervene. But I didn't, because you don't need rescuing, Erica." This time he did take one step in her direction. "That's been one of my mistakes all along. I keep trying to save you when you don't need saving. You're the strongest person I know. Nobody needs to bail you out of anything."

A knot formed in her throat so she couldn't force out any words as he continued slowly in her direction until he was directly in front of her, so close that she could see the bags under his eyes from obvious lack of sleep.

"Another of my mistakes was treating like you were disposable. Like you were just some girl at a club I could pick up and then go my way."

A tear trickled down her cheek and she looked away. Brock's gentle hand reached out and turned her back to face him. When she did, the look on his face took her breath away.

"Yet another of my mistakes was trying to buy you. Angie pointed that one out to me. You don't know too much about my family, but let's just say I got the idea that you had to bribe people to stick around," he said quietly. "Not that that excuses anything. You specifically asked me to stop, and I kept doing it, like the fat guy in there, only with cash."

At that, Erica managed to force out a few words. "You were an ass, but paying my father's medical bills hardly makes you Lardo."

"But my biggest mistake of all," Brock went on, "was letting you walk away without a fight. So I'm here to fight, Erica. And I'm going to keep fighting, until you agree me a second chance. To give us a second chance."

"Us?" she repeated, her voice suddenly cracking. "There is no—"

"Yeah, there is. There always was, from the time I hired you. We were a team in the office first, and then after that date, there definitely was even more. I just refused to see it. But I see it now."

Another tear slipped down her cheek and he leaned in to very gently brush it away with his lips, so gently that she trembled.

"How's your dad?" he asked.

Surprised, Erica murmured, "Doing all right. He has highs and lows. I should apologize too. He'd be dead if you hadn't helped us out financially, Brock. I'm sorry. Whatever your reasons were for giving me the money, it was still beyond generous. Thank you."

"How are you?" he asked, scanning her weary face.

"Burnt out," she admitted. "But I have a final job interview with Nico and Henderson on Friday. I think I may finally have a place at a job where I can actually use my degree."

The smile on Brock's face melted the ice that had surrounded Erica's heart for months and she sagged forward a little, just enough that he placed a hand on her waist.

"Good for you. I don't know how to say it without sounding

condescending, but I'm proud of you, Erica. You'll knock 'em dead."

She smiled, feeling the warm spread outward from the touch of his hand and sincere words. "Thanks. I'm proud of myself, frankly."

And then she hugged him hard. She didn't overthink it; she just did it because this was the man she'd love for what felt like forever, and he finally felt like he was on an even footing with her. Not a billionaire. Not her boss. Not her seducer. Just a man who had opened himself up to her and even asked about her life. A man who had let her fight her own battles and cheered her on when she won.

Brock's arms folded around her tightly and she leaned in closer, melting into the familiar heat of his embrace. "God, I missed this. I missed you so much."

"I missed you," he whispered in her ear. "And I love you, Erica."

"I love you," she whispered back, lifting her head to look into his eyes. "And next time, I give you permission to intervene if a lard ass is trying to feel me up."

Brock laughed and framed her face with his hands. "I promise I'll pound anyone who tries into the ground. I love you." He kissed her again, and then again, and then again, until Erica's weariness had completely burned away, replaced by the heat of Brock's hungry, tender kiss. "I love you. I love you," he whispered. "I love you now. I'll love you tomorrow. I'll love you forever. Give me six months and I'm going to ask you to marry me, Erica Samson."

"Why six months?" she asked giddily, matching him kiss for hungry kiss, almost climbing him in her need to be closer to him, skin to skin.

"Because I'd like to do some things differently in my own life, things that'll make you proud of me too," he said simply, before lifting her in his arms, carrying her to his car, and then whisking her off to his apartment and to bed.

And she knew without a doubt that when he asked someday, she'd say yes.

The End.

SIGN UP TO RECEIVE FREE BOOKS

S ign Up to Receive Free E-Books and Audiobook Codes.

Would you like to read **Savage Hearts** and **other romance books** for **free**?

You can sign up to receive free e-books and audiobooks by typing this link into your browser:

HTTPS://IVYWONDERSAUTHOR.COM/IVY-WONDERS-AUTHOR

©Copyright 2020 by Michelle Love - All rights Reserved
In no way is it legal to reproduce, duplicate, or transmit any part of this document in either electronic means or in printed format. Recording of this publication is strictly prohibited and any storage of this document is not allowed unless with written permission from the publisher. All rights are reserved.
Respective authors own all copyrights not held by the publisher.

❀ Created with Vellum

www.ingramcontent.com/pod-product-compliance
Lightning Source LLC
LaVergne TN
LVHW011737060526
838200LV00051B/3202